The Adventures of
Shamrock Sean

Shamrock Sean and the Wishing Well

Shamrock Sean and the Bird's Nest

Shamrock Sean Goes Fishing

Brian Gogarty

Illustrated by Roxanne Burchartz
of The Cartoon Saloon

THE O'BRIEN PRESS
DUBLIN

For my wife, Eileen, and children, Christine,
Nuala and Ryan, because they believe ...

This edition published 2010 by The O'Brien Press Ltd.
First published 2007 as three books:
Shamrock Sean and the Wishing Well
Shamrock Sean and the Bird's Nest
Shanrock Sean Goes Fishing
by The O'Brien Press Ltd
12 Terenure Road East, Rathgar, Dublin 6, D06 HD27, Ireland.
Tel: +353 1 4923333; Fax: +353 1 4922777
E-mail: books@obrien.ie
Website: www.obrien.ie
Reprinted 2012, 2014, 2015, 2016.

ISBN: 978-1-84717-192-4
Copyright for text © Brian Gogarty 2007
Copyright for typesetting, editing, layout design © The O'Brien Press Ltd

9 8 7 6
19 18 17 16

Editing, typesetting and design: The O'Brien Press Ltd
Printed and bound in Poland by Bialostockie Zaklady Graficzne S.A.
The paper in this book is produced using pulp from managed forests

The O'Brien Press receives assistance from

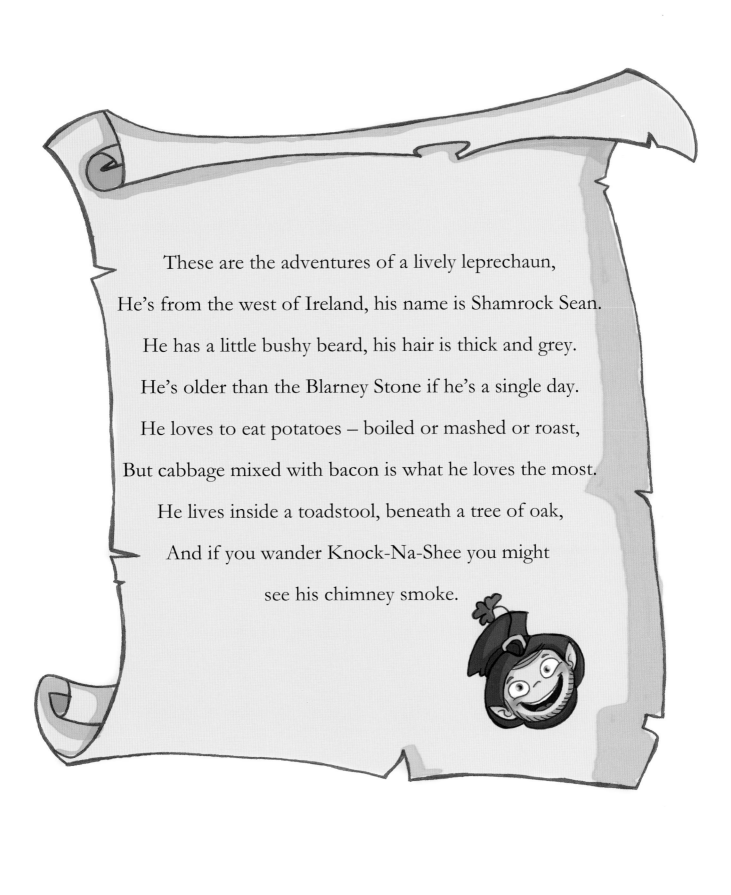

These are the adventures of a lively leprechaun,

He's from the west of Ireland, his name is Shamrock Sean.

He has a little bushy beard, his hair is thick and grey.

He's older than the Blarney Stone if he's a single day.

He loves to eat potatoes – boiled or mashed or roast,

But cabbage mixed with bacon is what he loves the most.

He lives inside a toadstool, beneath a tree of oak,

And if you wander Knock-Na-Shee you might

see his chimney smoke.

Shamrock Sean

and the Wishing Well

Shamrock Sean got out of bed

And rubbed his sleepy eyes.

He looked out of the window

At the clear blue sunny skies.

'It's such a lovely day,' he said,

I know just what I'll do.

I'll go down to the wishing well

And make a wish … or two.'

He ran across the meadow,

He ran right through the wood,

Until he reached the wishing well

And next to it he stood.

But he couldn't see inside,

For the wishing well was tall.

He said, 'It's not fair!

I'm really far too small.'

He moved a big square stone

And climbed up on the rim.

Then the silly leprechaun

Leaned over and **fell in!**

He shouted very loudly,

'Oh, someone help me, please!

I'm here inside the wishing well

With water to my knees.'

He got very cold and hungry

In that wishing well so deep.

He tried to climb the wall

But found it was too steep.

He waited and he waited,

It seemed like hours and hours.

Then suddenly he remembered

The wishing well's great powers.

Shamrock Sean closed his eyes

And wished with all his might.

'I wish that I was home,' he said.

– There was a flash of light.

At once he was back home again,

His feet still soaking wet.

'I wished and it came true!' he said,

'It's the best wish I've made yet.'

Shamrock Sean

and the Bird's Nest

One day in the springtime

Shamrock Sean worked near the hedge.

Digging in his garden,

He was planting greens and veg.

He leant upon his garden spade

To have a little rest,

And from the corner of his eye

He spied a small bird's nest.

He climbed between the branches

And stood upon one leg.

There, hidden down inside the nest,

He saw a single egg.

By a miracle of nature

The egg began to crack,

It made him lose his balance,

And he stumbled and fell back.

Just then the mother bird appeared

And said, 'What did you do?

My little egg's not due to hatch

For another day or two.'

Sean said, 'I just stood on the branch

To get a better view.

I didn't touch your little egg,

Honestly, it's true.'

'I must find worms,' said mother bird,

'But since he's newly born,

I can't go off in search of food

And leave him on his own.'

'I've got it! Don't you worry,'

responded Shamrock Sean.

'You stay here and leave the food

To this here Leprechaun.'

So Sean ran to his garden

Where the soil was freshly tilled.

He collected worms in handfuls

'Till a bucket load was filled.

He came back to the hungry chick

And said, 'I've worms galore.

If there's not enough to feed him,

I can get a whole lot more.'

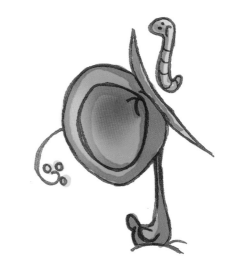

'Thank you, Sean, you're very kind,'

the mother bird then said.

And she lifted up a wing

To pat him gently on the head.

'I thought that leprechauns were mean,

Or so I have been told.

But now I know it isn't true –

you're worth your weight in gold.'

Shamrock Sean

Goes Fishing

Shamrock Sean went fishing

Down by the river's edge.

His rod was just a little stick

He'd found beside the hedge.

To it he tied a piece of string

And that would be the line.

His hook was just a safety pin,

But it would do just fine.

He put the stick between two stones,

He fixed it firm and tight.

Then lay down in the summer sun

And waited for a bite.

After many hours of waiting

The rod began to twitch.

Shamrock Sean said to himself –

This must be one big fish!

Or could it be a heavy boot?

Or might it be a rag?

But then he saw the safety pin

Had hooked a leather bag.

He opened up the bag

And could not believe his eyes.

For it was full of precious gems,

What a great surprise!

He put his hand into the bag

And moved it all about.

He found a note and trembled

As he read the message out:

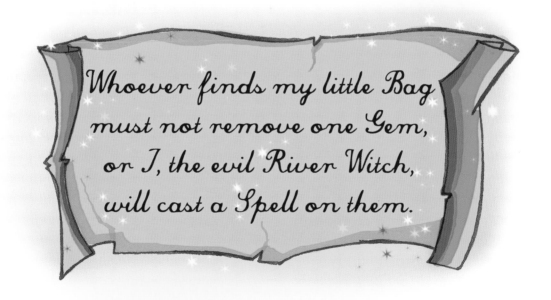

Whoever finds my little Bag
must not remove one Gem,
or I, the evil River Witch,
will cast a Spell on them.

Shamrock Sean is honest,

So he closed the bag up tight

And threw it back into the stream

With all his strength and might.

It hit the water with a splash

As he fell upon the ground.

Then a big fish grabbed his foot

And dragged him river-bound.

'Let me go,' cried Shamrock Sean.

He flapped his arms and screamed.

Then suddenly he woke up –

It had all been just a dream.

On the soft grass, in the sun,

Upon the bank so steep,

He'd rolled into the water

When he'd fallen fast asleep.

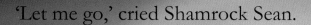

He crawled out of the water

And the rod began to twitch.

'Oh no!' he cried as he ran home.

'Here comes the River Witch!'